This Ladybird book belongs to

. . . .

For Mum, Dad and James
K.H.

LADYBIRD BOOKS
Ladybird Books is part of the Penguin Random House group of companies
whose addresses can be found at global.penguinrandomhouse.com.
www.penguin.co.uk   www.puffin.co.uk   www.ladybird.co.uk

Penguin
Random House
UK

First published 2021
002
Text and illustrations copyright © Kim Hillyard, 2021
The moral right of the author/illustrator has been asserted
Printed in Malaysia
A CIP catalogue record for this book is available from the British Library
ISBN: 978–0–241–41341–8
All correspondence to:
Ladybird Books, Penguin Random House Children's
One Embassy Gardens, 8 Viaduct Gardens
London SW11 7BW

MIX
Paper from
responsible sources
FSC® C018179
FSC
www.fsc.org

NED
and the
GREAT GARDEN
HAMSTER
RACE

Kim Hillyard

Today is the day Ned has been waiting for.

TODAY IS THE DAY OF... →

THE GREAT GARDEN HAMSTER RACE

Hamsters from all over the world have come to take part.

BIG
ONES

SMALL ONES

HAIRY ONES →

SCARY ONES ←

AND SOME VERY FAST-LOOKING ONES →

But Ned has been training and now

HE IS READY TO
WIN.

The race begins, and soon . . .

... Ned is in

FIRST PLACE!

He zooms past a little slug.

But Ned does not have time for small talk.

He races under some hungry pigeons.

But Ned does not have time to stop for lunch.

But Ned does not have time to stop and help.

He just runs and races . . .

and races and runs!

Until he slips and trips and falls into . . .

a **VERY** uncomfortable position!

And just when it seems like things cannot possibly
get any worse, he looks up and sees . . .

Now Ned is back on track.

But instead of running forward, he stops . . .

and thinks . . .

and decides to run . . .

. . . back to the giant hole . . .

back to the hungry pigeons . . .

. . . and back to the little slug!

Finally, Ned runs
to the finish line.

But it is a lot harder in the dark.

Suddenly, he looks up and sees . . .

A LIGHT!

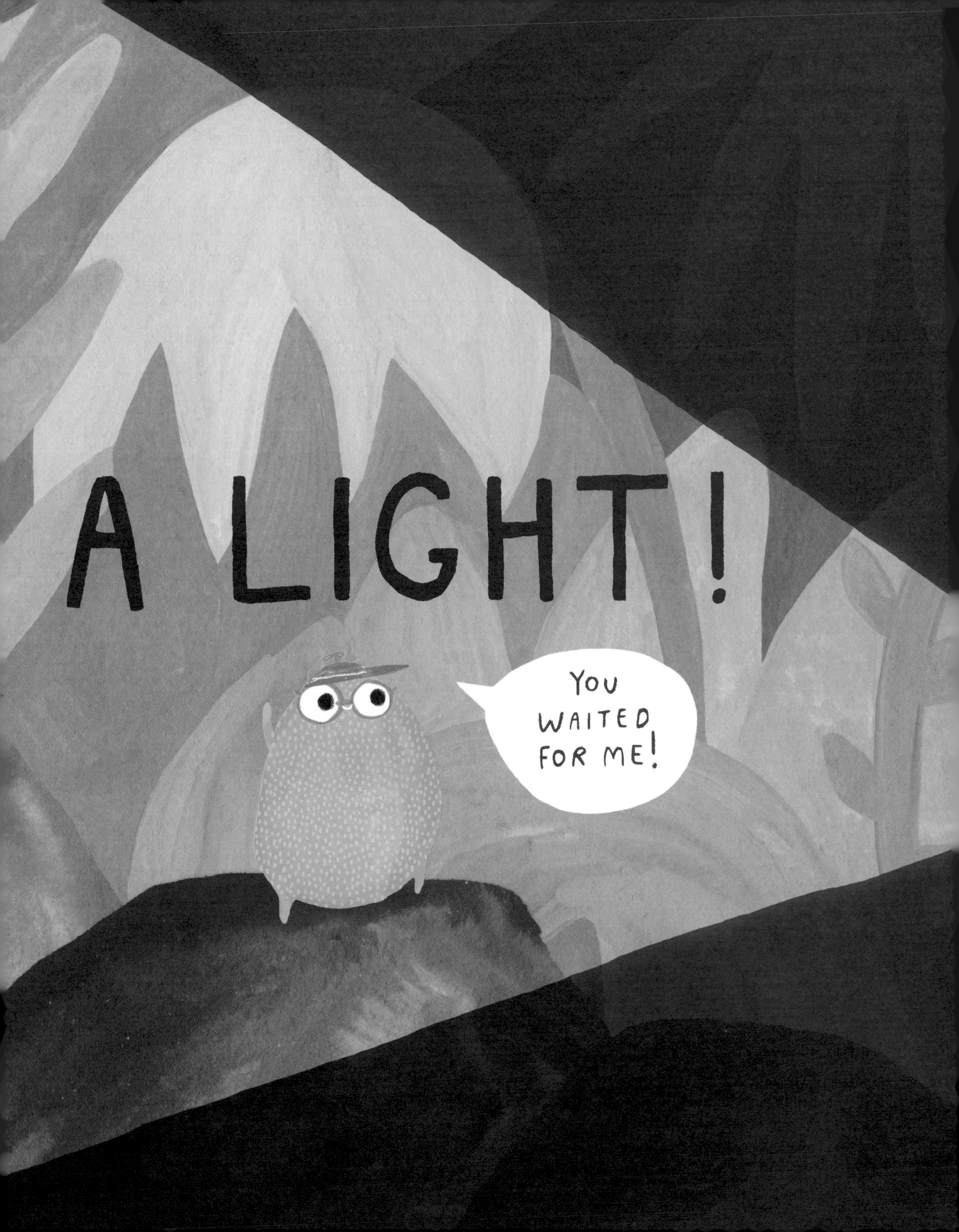

And so, with one giant leap,
the hamsters from all over the world
finished The Great Garden Hamster Race . . .